D01111894

248.4
Bla

C2

DISCARD

What It Means to Be
Called and Accountable

Henry Blackaby

Joyce Mitchell

DISCARD

Green Street Baptist Church
High Point, North Carolina

Woman's Missionary Union
Birmingham, Alabama

Woman's Missionary Union
P. O. Box 830010
Birmingham, AL 35283-0010

©1990 by Woman's Missionary Union

All rights reserved. Fourth printing 1991
Printed in the United States of America

Dewey Decimal Classification: 248.4
Subject Headings: CHRISTIAN LIFE
                  MINISTRY, CHRISTIAN

Scripture quotations indicated by NIV are from the Holy Bible, New
International Version. Copyright ©1973, 1978, 1984 International Bible
Society. Used by permission of Zondervan Bible Publishers.

Thomas Merton quote on page 46 is from Thomas Merton, *Contemplative
Prayer* (New York: Image Books, 1971), 41.

Called and Accountable (03292) is the text for a course in the subject area
Christian Growth and Service of the Church Study Course.

W913109•5M•1091

ISBN: 1-56309-000-7

CONTENTS

Part 1

INTRODUCTION

It is overwhelming to realize that the God of the Universe, the Creator of All That Is, calls each believer into a special relationship with Himself. This call and the relationship that follows are very personal and very real! The truth of this is found on almost every page of the Bible, in life after life, and verse after verse.

Even more amazing is the knowledge that God's choice to call people into such a personal relationship with Himself is that "He chose us in Him [Christ] before the creation of the world" (Eph. 1:4 NIV). He knew all about each of us before we were even formed in the womb (Psalm 139:13-16). When this truth grips a person's heart, he or she is never the same again. There comes into the life a deep sense of purpose from and stewardship to God.

Jeremiah was told: "Before I formed you in the womb I knew you, before you were born I set you apart" (Jer. 1:5 NIV). God then unfolded what this meant to Jeremiah, and it radically affected his life. And the Apostle Paul told that God had "set me apart from birth" (Gal. 1:15 NIV). Much of the book of Acts is the story of what this ultimately meant. Such love literally constrained Paul (constrain means to order all of the rest of his life). He became convinced that "He died for all, that those who live should no longer live for themselves but for Him who died for them and was raised again" (2 Cor. 5:15 NIV). And so deep was his sense of accountability before God that he said:

By the grace of God I am what I am, and his grace to me was not without effect. No, I worked harder than all of them—yet, not I, but the grace of God that was with me" (1 Cor. 15:10 NIV).

In the New Testament every believer is spoken of as the "called" of God, or the "chosen" of God, or "set apart" by God (Rom. 1:6; 1 Cor. 1:1-2; Eph. 1:1-6,18; 4:1; 1 Thess. 1:4; 2 Thess. 1:11; etc.). This truth, and its implications for each of our lives, will guide our study. But a key question at the beginning of our study is Why does God call us? The answer to this question will help us understand:

1. WHAT is a call?
2. WHO are the called?
3. HOW am I called?
4. WHEN am I called?
5. HOW do I live out the call?

Why does God call us?

First, the entire Bible bears witness to the truth that God, from eternity, chose to work through His people to accomplish His purposes in the world. He could have worked everything together Himself, but He chose not to do it that way. The Bible records how God called individuals into a special relationship with Himself at the very times He wanted to accomplish His purposes. When they understood His call and responded to Him, God did work through them mightily to accomplish His purposes.

Second, in understanding the call of God in our lives it is important to realize that God did not make us for time, but for eternity. We were created in His image (Gen. 1:26-30). This includes immortality (living for eternity). Jesus Himself declared constantly that the ones who believe in Him will have eternal life, and that we will reign with Him (Luke 22:29-30). Paul also confirmed this when he said that when God saved us, He raised us to sit in heavenly places in Christ Jesus (Eph. 2:6); and that we were "heirs of God and co-heirs with Christ" (Rom. 8:17 NIV). John declares that we shall "reign for ever and ever" (Rev. 22:5 NIV). Thus, God's goal is not time, but *eternity*. This life, then, is to prepare us for eternity. This was God's purpose from before the foundation of the world.

Third, God's goal is therefore to "conform us to the image of His Son" (Rom. 8:28-30 NIV). That is, He is seeking to develop *character*. It will be important at this time in our study to place clearly before us this passage in Romans: "We know that in all things God works for the good of those who love Him, who have been called according to His purpose. For those God foreknew he also predestined to be conformed to the likeness of His Son. . . . And those he predestined, he also called; those he called, he also justified; those he justified, he also glorified."

This truth carries with it so much of the why of our being called of God. Such character is developed in the crucible of relationship with Him in our world as He works out in our life His eternal plan of redemption. He calls us into a relationship with Himself, so in that relationship we can come to know him and experience His working in us and through us. In that relationship, and only there, does He develop character in us in preparation for an eternity with Him. This may sound to you at this time in our study very "heavy." It is—but it is the heart of the Christian's life!

The entire process of developing such Christlike character in us begins when God calls us to Himself, for a relationship of love. This love relationship continues throughout the rest of life, as God develops us, equips us, and takes us with Him on His redemptive mission in our world. We could study any of the persons in the Bible and see this unfolding. But we will take only one example, the disciples Jesus called. Jesus called His disciples and said, "Follow me." And they immediately left all and followed Him. Jesus knew it was now His assignment from the Father to prepare them for a world missions task. He fulfilled that work of training them. What this involved is clearly stated in His prayer in John 17.

> I have revealed you to those whom you gave me out of the world. They were yours; you gave them to me and they have obeyed your word. Now they know that everything you have given me comes from you. For I gave them the words you gave me and they accepted them. They knew with certainty that I came from you, and they believed that you sent me (John 17:6-8 NIV).

The Son of God had the assignment from the Father to call specific men into a relationship with Himself; then He was to share His life with them, teaching them and guiding them and molding them as the Father had instructed Him until they knew the Father and responded to Him. The more they responded to Him, the more God used them to go with His risen, living Son on a redemptive mission to the ends of the earth. As they did, God turned a world upside down through their lives.

With this pattern in mind, we must now ask, Why does God call us? It is so we can come to know and experience Him mightily working in us and through us, developing in us Christlikeness of character in preparation for an eternity with Him. All this He does because He loves us!

Chapter 1

What Is a Call?

This call is to a RELATIONSHIP. Often we think of being saved as simply being able to go to heaven when we die. All through the Bible, and especially in the New Testament, salvation is primarily being called by God to be in a saving relationship with Him. This is a relationship of love and comes through having a relationship with His Son. From the very beginning in the Garden of Eden the picture is that of God calling to Adam and Eve for relationship (Gen. 3:9). Sin had broken the relationship of love. The rest of the Bible is the story of God pursuing the relationship of love. In every generation God has actively called His people to a redemptive relationship with Himself. God then provided salvation through His Son, so the relationship with Him could be restored. This is why the testimonies of the great servants of God always tell of the overwhelming relationship of love that took place when they were saved. God met them and in love saved them. And now a love relationship has been established that will last forever. But there is also another aspect of this relationship and calling, which is so often overlooked or neglected.

This relationship is always REDEMPTIVE. The call to salvation is at the same time a call to be on mission with God in our world. This truth is expressed throughout the entire Bible, and those mightily used of God throughout history all bear witness to the reality of this. Almost from the moment of salvation there comes over the Christian a deep sense of being on mission with the Lord in our world.

ALL are called. It is so important to realize that every

Christian is called by God when they are saved. Peter, preaching on the day of Pentecost, said to the crowds who heard him, and were convicted, "'Repent and be baptized, every one of you, in the name of Jesus Christ for the forgiveness of your sins. And you will receive the gift of the Holy Spirit. The promise is for you and your children and for all who are far off—for all whom the Lord our God will call'" (Acts 2:38-39 NIV). Paul, speaking to the church at Rome, said, "And you also are among those who are called to belong to Jesus Christ. To all in Rome who are loved by God and called to be saints" (Rom. 1:6-7 NIV). Becoming a Christian in the New Testament is described as being called by God into a relationship with Him through His Son. Paul, with excitement, adds:

> Continue to work out your salvation with fear and trembling, for it is God who works in you to will and to act according to his good purpose" (Phil. 2:12-13 NIV).

What he meant was each one of you must let the full implication of your salvation work itself out into every area of your life. Each of you must respond to Him as Lord over all your life. For it is He now Who will be working in your life, causing you to want to do His will, and then working in your life to enable you to do it. What an exciting possibility for every Christian!

Peter also tells us that every Christian is specially chosen by God.

> You are a chosen people, a royal priesthood, a holy nation, a people belonging to God" (1 Peter 2:9 NIV).

Not one is excluded! Every Christian is chosen and called by God!

Gerry came from a Roman Catholic background. He was a university student in the city where I pastored. A friend of Gerry, who had become a Christian and was now a member of our church, helped Gerry become a Christian. From the beginning of his Christian life Gerry lived with a deep inner sense of a call to be on mission with his Saviour. Within a few weeks he came forward weeping, saying, "God wants me to be fully available to Him. Today I release my life to do anything that needs to be done. Is there some need that I can meet?"

That very week I had received an urgent call from our Indian pastor in Cochin, expressing a need for a Sunday School teacher. I shared that need and Gerry eagerly agreed to drive the 120 miles one way each Sunday. He did this for several years, taking other students to help him. Then the old Indian pastor's health broke and he had to return to the US.

The Indian people asked Gerry to be their pastor. His servant heart responded to their need, and for several years he pastored those people. Gerry and his wife, Connie, completed university, and then study at Golden Gate Baptist Theological Seminary. While there another urgent call came for someone with a Roman Catholic and French background to anchor our work in Quebec, a French Catholic province. Again Gerry saw his life as totally available to God and responded. Gerry and Connie and their three children are serving faithfully in Montreal, Quebec, in our Southern Baptist work, their lives fully open to God's daily call on them.

Throughout the Bible, and throughout history, those mightily used of God have had this same pattern in their lives. My own life began with a deep sense that God had something in mind when He saved me (see John 15:16 for this truth). Anything that God presented to me I responded to Him as His servant. I led youth, I taught and watched for anything God would desire to do through my life. Then a church asked if I would be their music/education director. It never crossed my mind not to respond for I knew that the call to salvation was at the same time the call to serve with God in my world.

That same church two years later asked if I would be their pastor. I did, and served for five years. Later some churches asked if I would be their director of missions. I did, and served for six years. Then the Home Mission Board asked if I would guide our Convention toward prayer and spiritual awakening. I did, and have now served for more than two years.

Every Christian is called of God to salvation, and in that

same call is the call to be on mission with God in our world. This is what it means to be called. God is seeking to bring a lost world back to Himself. He loves every person. He is not willing that any should perish. He has always been working in our world to seek and to save those who are lost. That is what He was doing when He called you! Those He saves, He involves as fellow workers with Himself (1 Cor. 3:9) in His eternal purpose to save a lost world. In every generation, in every place He saves some, develops them as His children, and takes them on mission with Him in their world. This is what it means to be called.

In this entire process God takes the initiative to come to His people and to let them know what He is doing or about to do. He came to Noah at the moment He was about to judge the world by a flood. Unless God had come to him, Noah could not have known what was about to happen. But that Noah did know meant that God wanted to accomplish His purpose through Noah. So God gave Noah an assignment, and Noah responded as a co-worker with God.

When God was about to free 2 1/2 million of His people from the slavery in Egypt, He took the initiative to come to Moses and let Moses know what He was about to do. This revelation was God's invitation for Moses to work with Him to accomplish His purposes for His people. God came this way to each of the prophets.

To the disciples Jesus said, "You did not choose me, but I chose you and appointed you to go and bear fruit—fruit that will last" (John 15:16 NIV), to the Apostle Paul, and to His people throughout history. This pattern is found every time God is about to do a great work in our world, and it is still true today! It is true right now for your life also!

This call of God will always involve some kind of major adjustment in your life to be the person God can use to accomplish His purposes. Moses had to leave herding sheep. David could not keep doing what he was doing and be king at the same time. The disciples of Jesus could no longer continue fishing and go with Jesus at the same time. So it has always been: Lawyers, doctors, schoolteachers, truck drivers, salespeople, nurses, bankers, etc., when they become

Christians, respond to Him as Lord over all of their lives, so He can accomplish His plans through His people.

One of the greatest developments today is the tremendous number of missions volunteers who are leaving all, and following Jesus—across America and around the world. Teachers are going into China, so that our Lord can reach Chinese through them; business people are making their lives available through their business connections around the world, so Christ can bring lost persons to Himself who would not hear any other way. Tens of thousands of volunteers are going around the world each year with a deep sense of being on mission with their Lord!

What a difference this is making in our generation. A young woman doctor recently gave the first years of her practice to go and work in Yemen while her husband served as a teacher in the school. They will never be the same again, and people have heard the gospel who would not otherwise have heard. The call to salvation is a call to go on mission with our Lord in our world. But none have gone without major adjustments in their lives. Some had to give up their successful medical or legal practice; others had to leave aging parents; others had to risk their health and their children; still others had to learn new languages and adapt to strange customs and cultures. But God has no other way to reach a lost world, except through those He calls to become His children through faith in His Son. Such love is what God counts on to move us to go with Him into our lost world.

One final response always accompanies God's call—OBEDIENCE! Once as a child of God you know an initiative of God in your life, you must immediately, and without resistance or discussion, respond obediently to all God is directing. Only then will you experience God's working mightily through your life. This was true in the life of Hudson Taylor. He was training as a medical doctor. When God made it unmistakably clear that He wanted to reach the peoples of inland China with the gospel, and do it through Taylor's life, obedience was all that was left for him. He was obedient, and God did reach hundreds of thousands, even millions, of precious Chinese people through Hudson Taylor's life and those God would bring alongside of him to preach, teach, and heal in China.

Further, a call always involves the person in the corporate life of the people of God. Your life, as God calls you, will become vitally involved with all the members in your church family. It may bring your life also into a vital relation with the other churches of your association; and you may find your life working alongside of the larger family called Southern Baptists throughout the world. The call of God is always a call to the whole world through all of His people.

Chapter 2

Who Are the Called?

You may still be asking, "But just who are the called? Are they a special group of persons? What about my life? Am I called too? How would I know? What would it sound like?" And sincerely your heart may be saying, "Lord, I do love You! I do belong to You! I am Your servant, and I truly want to serve You! But, Lord, am I really called to be on mission with you in my world? Lord, just who are the called?"

All Christians are called, as we have already noted. Let's look briefly at some Scripture passages that assure us that *all of us*, each of us, is called. In Exodus 19, when God first put a special nation together through whom He would bring salvation to the whole world, He said, "'I carried you on eagle's wings and brought you to myself. Now if you obey me fully and keep my covenant, then out of all nations you will be my treasured possession. Although the whole earth is mine, you will be for me a kingdom of priests and a holy nation'" (Ex. 19:4-6 NIV). He said they would be a kingdom of priests—not a kingdom with a priesthood. Each of them, and all of them, would be priests unto God. The Levites would be the ones assigned to train and equip the entire nation to walk with God as priests unto God, so He could fulfill His purposes to save the nations of the world through them. This same truth is stated in the New Testament.

> You also, like living stones, are being built into a spiritual house to be a holy priesthood, offering spiritual sacrifices acceptable to God through Jesus Christ.
> You are a chosen people, a royal priesthood, a holy nation, a people belonging to God, that you may declare the praises of him

11

who called you out of darkness into his wonderful light. Once you were not a people, but now you are the people of God, once you had not received mercy, but now you have received mercy (1 Peter 2.5,9-10 NIV).

Each believer is called of God and is to function before God and a watching world as a priest unto God. God, therefore, promised that He would enable every believer to function this way by the empowering presence of His Holy Spirit. At Pentecost God fulfilled that promise, and Peter announced to a deeply affected world:

This is what was spoken by the prophet Joel: "In the last days, God says, I will pour out my Spirit on all people. Your sons and daughters will prophesy, your young men will see visions, your old men will dream dreams. Even on my servants, both men and women, I will pour out my Spirit in those days" (Acts 2:16-18 NIV).

Notice the extensiveness and completeness of God's call and God's equipping all people, sons, daughters, young men, old men, and both men and women. This includes your life also.

It is also interesting and encouraging to realize that throughout the Bible most of those God calls and works through mightily are what we today would call laypeople. They were very ordinary people called and enabled by God to work with Him in their world. Their abilities or skills were not as important as their relationship with God. Their heart relationship of love and trust in God always determined how much God was able to do through them.

I remember Arthur and Marion. They were in their 70s when they came to me as their pastor to say they felt God wanted to use them in starting a mission church in a Russian community. Arthur had been an accountant all his life. He had been a deacon, and she had always served faithfully by his side. Now God was asking them in retirement to be available to Him for His larger purposes.

Arthur took 16 courses from the seminary extension department and received his pastoral ministries certificate in preparation for serving as our mission pastor. They served for six years, winning many scores of people to the Lord in one of the most difficult communities around us. We ordained Arthur at age 76. That year he also taught younger men in our theological college in the area of accounting and finances. That year he died of cancer, believing that the best years of their lives were the last years as God worked through them to win a lost world to Himself. They were just ordinary Christians who were also available, and God worked through them.

Alex worked in a steel plant, but God worked in his life to do church planting also. Alex and Eileen made their lives available to God and were used wonderfully to begin a new mission church in a needy community.

Melvin worked for Sears for 26 years and his wife was a practical nurse. In their 50s they sensed God wanted them to use the next years of their lives in missions. They volunteered to be dorm parents for missionaries' kids (MKs) in Zambia. They were accepted, and spent the next eight years building the residence and caring for the children. Melvin also direct-ed a successful Bible correspondence course which enrolled over 100,000 persons, with thousands of people coming to know Christ as their Saviour. All these examples are ordinary people who knew that God has a right to use their lives in His time and place, and they responded.

You may be thinking that you are not equipped to do this. Remember, in John 17 Jesus revealed to us that the Father gives our lives to Him for Jesus to develop and teach us and to make us useful vessels that His Father can use to save a lost and dying world. In that significant prayer, Jesus said to the Father:

> Father . . . I have brought you glory on earth by completing the work you gave me to do. . . . I have revealed you to those whom you gave me out of the world. They were yours; you gave them to me and they have obeyed your word. Now they know that everything you have given me comes from you. For I gave them the words you gave me and they accepted them. They knew with certainty that I came from you, and they believed that you sent

me. . . . I have given them the glory that you gave me . . . to let the world know that you sent me, and have loved them even as you have loved me (John 17:1,4,6-8,22-23 NIV).

When Jesus called the first disciples, He assured them of His responsibility for their lives by saying to them, "'Come, follow me . . . and I will make you'" (Mark 1:17 NIV). Again He said to them, "This is the will of him who sent me, that I should lose none of all that he has given me" (John 6:39 NIV). All of the Gospels record how Jesus taught, trained, guided, encouraged, empowered, and fully equipped His disciples for all God had in mind to do through them. John 17 reveals just how thoroughly Jesus prepared them for their mission in their world. Included in that very prayer in John 17 is your life and mine.

As Jesus said, "'My prayer is not for them alone. I pray also for those who will believe in me through their message'" (John 17:20 NIV). So you need not be concerned that you are not prepared to be of use to God. Our living Lord has accepted your life from the Father and is at work "making you to become" all God wants you to be.

Each one of us is important to God! We are ordinary people who love God with all our hearts, and who know that the call to salvation is also a call to be laborers together with God in our world. As we respond to the call of God in a yieldedness to Him, He powerfully accomplishes His purpose to save a lost world through our lives. God seeks out those who are willing to "stand before Him . . . on behalf of the land" (Ezek. 22:30-31 NIV). If He cannot find one, the land and the people are destroyed. But when He does find someone who will "go for us" (Isa. 6:8 NIV), He is able to save multitudes of people (study Jonah, Esther, and the book of Acts). He says His "eyes . . . range throughout the earth to strengthen those whose hearts are fully committed to him" (2 Chron. 16:9 NIV).

So deep is the love of God for our lost world that the Spirit of God "works in you to will and to act according to his good purpose" (Phil. 2:13 NIV). Do you sense that the Spirit of God is working in your life, causing you to want to do His will and promising to help you to accomplish His will?

Jerry and Brenda had not been married long. Jerry had just become a Christian. As they studied their Bible, seeking to be faithful children of God, they realized that they must be as prepared and as available to God as possible. This is what the Scriptures revealed to them. They came to attend the theological college we had established in our church to gain some basic knowledge of God and His Word. As they studied, God saw their hearts, and through unusual circumstances led them to respond to an Indian reservation to teach the Bible. They completed their three years of study, and by then God had established them with a heart for the Indian people and the special skill to enable them to minister to them.

God reached many of the Indian people for the Lord through Jerry and Brenda. Later they were called to pastor an Indian mission. Now Jerry directs the work for the reaching of all the Indian people in Canada, for Canadian Southern Baptists, and is training many Indian people who are themselves being called to reach their own people. Two lives called to salvation, but realizing that the call to salvation was a call to be fully available to God for His greater purposes to win a lost world wherever He would choose to send them. What a difference they have made. And what a sense of purpose has captured their lives too.

Chapter 3

How Am I Called?

For a Christian to ask seriously the question How am I called?, the Christian must bring with this question a personal commitment both to respond and to be accountable to God in the calling. When Christians sense that God is guiding them to a clear, simple answer to this question, they will also be deeply aware (even painfully aware) that having the knowledge of His will brings with it immediately a solemn sense of accountability.

When you sense God is calling you, you can never be the same again! You will have to say, "Yes, Lord!" Be aware that you may tend to say no. But you cannot say, "No, Lord!" For if you say no at that moment He is no longer Lord. For lordship means, by definition, always a yes. When Jesus is Lord, His servant always says, "Yes, Lord!"

We have already indicated that the initial call is a call to salvation, a call to become a child of God and servant of Jesus Christ. It is an eternal decision and an eternal relationship. But from that moment when I am born again, how am I called by God in my mission with Him?

First, remember that when you are born again as a child of God, you are given spiritual senses (Matt. 12:11-23), so you can hear and see and understand all the ways and activities of God. But you must develop your spiritual senses by use (Heb. 5:13-14). As a child is fully equipped with physical senses to function fully and well in the physical world, so the Christian is given spiritual senses to function in the spiritual world, in our relationship with God. We can learn to hear His voice (John 10:2-4,27) and follow Him; we can learn to see His activity and join Him (John 3:3; 5:17; 19-20), and we can learn to understand with our hearts and obey Him (John 14:26; 16:13-15).

Just as a little child learns to function in our world a little at a time, if we are faithful in a little, He will give us more (Luke 16:10). Jesus said that when we hear and then obey, we are like a man building his house on a rock—nothing can shake it or destroy it (Luke 6:46-49).

There are some things that must be firmly in place in the Christian's life to experience the fullness of God's calling in life.

1. A person must clearly and unmistakably *know* Him. Jesus said eternal life was coming to "know you, the only true God, and Jesus Christ, whom you have sent" (John 17:3 NIV). This means you clearly have come to receive Jesus Christ into your life as your personal Saviour and Lord.

2. Simply, as a child, you must daily *believe* Him; that is, you accept as true all He has revealed about Himself (in His Word, the Bible) and accept as binding upon your life all He has said, asked, or commanded. If He is Who He says He is, you believe Him.

3. With all the heart, mind, soul, and strength, you *love* and *trust* Him. You must respond unconditionally to Him. His love will constrain you (2 Cor. 5:14).

4. Unhesitantly and immediately you will *obey* Him. Jesus said, "'If anyone loves me, he will obey my teaching. My Father will love him, and we will come to him and make our home with him. He who does not love me will not obey my teaching'" (John 14:23-24 NIV).

In the midst of your life the Holy Spirit, your enabler, will assist you in hearing and knowing the call and will of God. He will do this all through your life (John 14:25-26; 16:13-15; Rom. 8:26; 1 Cor. 2:10-16).

Our oldest son Richard first came to know the Lord as a young boy. We were confident that if we would instruct him to listen to the Lord, and if we would create the spiritual atmosphere in which God could speak to him, that Richard would respond.

While a teenager he came forward in a worship service saying, "Dad, I've known that God was calling me, but I have been running from the Lord. I come now to say yes to God's call for me to be His servant. I think I might be a pastor."

He then began answering God's continuing call by serving as president of the youth group, as Baptist Student Ministry (BSM) president, and then BSM state president. After graduation he went to seminary, being called of God to Southwestern Baptist Theological Seminary. Then a further call came to enter the PhD program and write a history of Canadian Southern Baptist work. Now he has responded to God's call to pastor Friendship Baptist Church in Winnipeg, Manitoba, Canada.

He continues to experience daily the call of God in his life; aided, taught, and enabled to do it by the Spirit of God. As a matter of fact, all five of our children (four boys and one girl) have sensed the call of God to ministry or missions, and continue to openly respond to God's daily claim on their lives.

It is within the family and within the church family that the spiritual atmosphere is created where the ordinary Christian can hear the call of God and respond confidently. It is here that the call of God is clarified and the Christian assisted to obey God's call. The missions organizations of the church have a key role in creating this spiritual atmosphere, so that *every* believer can understand and experience his or her calling and carry it out in a responsible and effective way. The missions organizations provide opportunities for Bible study, mission study, missions activities, personal involvement, models for missions, and ministry and service opportunities. It is therefore in the midst of serving our Lord that His call is clarified. When His call is clarified, we can respond with obedience!

Linda and Renee came to our association as US-2 missionaries. They had sensed the call of God to come and spend two years with us. During these two years, we sought to create a spiritual atmosphere in which God could have the maximum opportunity to reveal to each of them the next step in His claim on and call for their lives. We spent time in Bible study and answering questions. They were given assignments that they sensed were from the Lord, and they responded eagerly. We walked with them through the disappointments, failures, victories, and the painful and happy times.

Their assignment ended in the fall of 1986. Renee went on to other missions assignments and is now completing seminary training in preparation for a life of ministry. Linda went on to direct the Southern Baptist witness to the Winter Olympics in Calgary, Alberta, then to serve in New York, and is now taking seminary courses in the Northeast in preparation for a life of being on mission with her Lord.

The how of being called of God came for both Renee and Linda in the midst of their personal relationship with God and His people as they followed their Lord daily.

Chapter 4

When Am I Called?

The Bible reveals, as we study carefully the lives of those God used significantly, that it is when we are in the midst of God's activity in our world that we most clearly know the call of God for our lives. A most significant verse to help us understand this is found in the life and witness of Jesus. He said:

> "My Father is always at His work to this very day, and I, too, am working. . . . The Son can do nothing of Himself [on His own initiative]; he can do only what he sees His Father doing, because whatever the Father does the Son also does. For the Father loves the Son and shows Him all He does" (John 5:17,19-20 NIV).

First, Jesus said that it was the Father Who was at work in the world. Jesus was His servant. Jesus said the servant does not take the initiative, but rather watches to see where the Father (Master) is working and joins Him. But Jesus said the Father loves the Son, and therefore shows Him everything that He Himself is doing. The Son joins in with the Father, working together with Him. It is then that the Father is able to complete all He has purposed to do through the Son; i.e., bring a lost world back to Himself. He does it through His Son Who loves, trusts, and obeys the Father.

Every person through whom God is able to work mightily has lived out this kind of relationship with God. Amos, the prophet, was a layman (a shepherd and a caretaker of sycamore-fig trees). He said, "'I was neither a prophet nor a prophet's son. . . . But the Lord took me . . . and said to me,

"Go, prophesy to my people"'" (Amos 7:14-15 NIV). Amos responded obediently, and God accomplished His purposes through him. This same pattern is seen in Jeremiah (Jer. 1:4-12), in Moses (Ex. 3:15); the Judges, David, all the prophets, the disciples, the Apostle Paul, and God's people throughout history. This process continues to this very day, and is the way God will call and work through your life too.

When God sees a growing, loving, and responsive relationship of trust in Him in one of His children, He continues His call to that person, usually in the midst of his or her daily routine, to a special and deeper relationship with Him. In each life that He calls the daily positive response of the person brings the enabling presence and power of the Spirit of God to accomplish his or her assignment with God. For example, God placed His Spirit on the responsive Moses and the 70 elders who were to work with him (Num. 11:16-25); God's Spirit enabled the workmen who were to build the tabernacle (Ex. 35:30 to 36:1); the Judges who were called by God to be deliverers for His people (Judg. 3:10; 6:34; 11:29; 13:25; 14:6,19; 15:14); David (1 Sam. 16:13); the disciples at Pentecost (Acts 2:1-4); and the Apostle Paul (Acts 9:15-19).

This has been true of every servant God has used mightily in history. You can count on His presence and power in your life also when you respond in obedience to serve the Lord as He calls your life to be on mission with Him in your world. The Spirit-filled life was to be God's normal life for the Christian (1 Cor. 12:13; Eph. 5:18; 1 John 4:13). As each believer seeks to follow the Lord Who has called him, the Holy Spirit teaches him and guides him (John 14:26; 16:13-15); helps him when he prays (Rom. 8:26); and helps him to know all the things that are freely given to him by God (1 Cor. 2:10-16).

A Christian will also know when she is being called by God, as she functions in the life of His church (the body of Christ). The most complete picture of the body working together is found in 1 Corinthians 12 and Ephesians 4. Each member in the body functions where God places him or her in the body, and each assists the other parts of the body to grow up into the Head, which is Christ. This is not merely a figure of speech, it is a living reality. The loving Christ is truly present in the church body, and each member really does assist the others to know and do the will of God. Paul constantly affirmed his need of other believers helping him know and carry out the call of God in his life (Rom. 1:11 12, Eph. 6:19-20). In the church where God places you He has provided other believers whom He has equipped to assist you in knowing God's activity in your life, and whom God has chosen to assist you in carrying out His will. Your life in the body is crucial if God is to carry out His eternal purpose for your life today.

This will involve you not only in your church family but also with the other churches in your local association (as happened in the New Testament), across the nation, and around the world. God's call is to take the gospel to every person and into every nation. God's plan for accomplishing this is to call your life to Himself, and then place your life alongside all the others He has called, so that together, as one people, He can work dramatically across an entire world through you!

On a personal level, God will affirm His call in your life when you (1) spend personal time with God in His Word (the Scriptures), (2) spend time with God in prayer, (3) look to see the activities of God around your life, (4) listen to the voice of God as you live out your life in the midst of His people in your church.

Chapter 5

How Do I Live Out the Call?

God Himself places within the heart of every believer the deepest desire to be experiencing the strong presence and power of God working in him and through him (Phil 2:12-13). But how does one come to experience in life the deep reality of being called and accountable? As we look at the answer to this question, it is important to remember that not only is it "God who works in you to will and to act according to His good purpose" (Phil 2:13 NIV) but also "he who began a good work in you will carry it on to completion until the day of Christ Jesus" (Phil 1:6 NIV). These two truths carry with them enormous implications!

First, as a Christian living in the world, God is actively at work in your life at the moment you begin to sense an inner desire to do the will of God. This is the activity of God in your life causing you to want to do His will. The activity of God may be experienced while you are studying the Bible; or when you are worshiping in your church; or when you are praying; or in the midst of your daily routine; or even when you are talking with a friend or one of your family. There are some things that only God can do.

Bill and Anne responded very differently from other people when the city learned that a mounted policeman had been murdered. The two young men who committed the crime were arrested, and the anger of the people in the city mounted. But during our prayer meeting Bill and Anne began to weep as they shared a deep burden in their hearts for the parents of the two young men arrested. They themselves had a son in jail and they knew the pain and loneliness of being the parents. As they shared their hearts, the entire church family began to understand and feel their pain too.

They asked that we pray for them as they invited the parents of these two boys to their home for coffee and let them know of their personal love and concern. We did.

These parents said, "We have been hated and cursed by others. You are the only persons who have cared about our hurt. Thank you!"

Out of this experience our church family, along with Bill and Anne, began an extensive jail ministry—to both the inmates and the parents and family in several jails and prisons. The entire church became involved because two believers knew they were children of a loving God and knew that God was calling them to respond to what He wanted to do through them and their church for others who were hurting.

Cathy joined our church. The prayer meeting became a very special place for her, for it was as she prayed that she often sensed the moving of God in her life giving her clear directions.

One Wednesday evening she shared, "God has given me a great burden for ministering to the mentally retarded and their families. I grew up with a mentally retarded sister. I know what this does to the parents and the family. No one in the churches of our city is ministering to these. I sense we should seek God's guidance to see if we should be involved." The more she shared and the more we prayed, the more our hearts came together as one (Matt. 18:19-20).

We became convinced that God was directing not only Cathy but our entire church to become involved. To us it was a clear call of God, and we felt accountable to God to respond. We did, and Cathy helped us know what to do. Soon we were having 15 to 20 mentally retarded young adults attending, and some of their family members. Our church came to experience more of the meaning of pure love through these special people than we had ever experienced before. God called Cathy and her church as she prayed (and then we prayed with her), and God began to accomplish His loving purposes through us.

Terry worked in a very significant microchip company. As he studied his Bible and prayed and worshipped regularly, God began to speak to him. During a worship service, Terry came forward indicating that God was calling him to be a more effective witness in his place of work.

"But," he said, "my desk is out of the way at the end of a hall, and only one person comes by my office. How can God use me to witness to the many in my office?"

I shared his sense of call with the church family, and we pledged to pray with him. I encouraged him to look for the activity of God in answer to our prayer and be prepared to obey immediately. It was not long before he joyfully shared the following with the church: "This week my boss came to me and said, 'Terry, I want to move your desk. I hope you don't mind!' My desk now is in the busiest place in the office, right at the drinking fountain, the copier, and the coffee center. Everybody comes by my desk now. Please pray for me that I will be the faithful witness God has called me to be!"

How do you live out the call of God in your life? It is done in your daily relationship with God, from the beginning of the day to the end of the day! In your quiet time alone with God at the beginning of the day God speaks to you and guides you to understand and know what He is planning to do that day, where He has your life.

If you close this time by saying, "O God, please go with me this day and bless me!" God may say to us, "You have it backwards! I have a will and plan for what I want to do through your life today. I want you to go with Me. So I am alerting you through My Word and your praying to know My will for you, so you can be partners with Me today!"

In your same quiet time the Lord Jesus will bring to your heart the full assurance that whatever the Father has in mind, He (Jesus) will be present with you and in you to provide all the resources you will need to fulfill the Father's will. In addition to that, the Holy Spirit will be giving His assurance that

He will enable you to implement in your life the will of God and any call of God! What an incredible privilege! What an awesome responsibility! What an accountability we have to love Him, believe Him, trust Him, and obey Him. It is then that you will experience the wonderful presence and power of God working His will in you and through you.

Second, because you know that God is working in you and will complete what He has begun, you should live with a clear sense of expectation and anticipation of God's doing this in your life daily! It is not what you can do for God, but what God is doing in you! And what He begins, He Himself will bring to completion! God spoke through His prophet Isaiah, saying:

> I make known the end from the beginning, from ancient times, what is still to come. I say: My purpose will stand, and I will do all that I please. . . . What I have said, that will I bring about; what I have planned, that will I do" (Isa. 46:10-11 NIV).

How encouraging it is to read again in Isaiah, a promise from God:

> "Surely, as I have planned, so it will be, and as I have purposed, so it will stand. . . . For the Lord Almighty has purposed, and who can thwart Him? His hand is stretched out, and who can turn it back?" (Isa. 14:24,27 NIV).

Once God has spoken to your heart, it is as good as done. For He has never spoken to reveal His will and not Himself guaranteed the completion of what He has said. This will be as true in your life as in the lives of any in the Bible or history. You might want to study for yourself the following additional Scripture passages to give yourself further encouragement: Isaiah 55:8ff.; Numbers 23:19; Hebrews 13:20-21.

Third, it will be important to recognize the activity, or working of God, in your life, so you can quickly join Him. Jesus made this very clear in His own relationship with the Father when He said:

> "My Father is always at work to this very day, and I, too, am working. . . . The Son can do nothing by Himself [on His own ini-

tiative]; he can do only what He sees the Father doing, because whatever the Father does the Son does. For the Father loves the Son and shows him all He does" (John 5:17,19-20 NIV).

You might ask, How would I recognize the Father's activity? Let me help you, from the life of Jesus. In John 6:44,45,65, Jesus said that no one would come to Him unless the Father drew and taught them. But those in whose life the Father was working would come to Him. Jesus, therefore, would look for such drawing in the lives of those around Him. For instance, when He saw Zacchaeus up a tree, He might have said to Himself, "No one could seek after Me with that kind of earnestness unless My Father was at work in his life. I've got to join My Father's activity." So he left the crowd and went to his house, and salvation came to Zacchaeus that night!

Sherri, a nurse at our university, asked the church to pray that God would help her witness at school. She felt God had called her not only to be a nurse but to witness to others. But she did not know just where. I, as her pastor, shared these Scripture passages with her and encouraged her to look for the "activity of God—things only God could do" that were happening around her life, and then be ready to let her life be available for God to use. She came back to the church excited, saying, "A girl who has been in classes with me for two years came up to me and said, 'I think you might be a Christian. I need to talk to you.' I joined her, and she said, 'Eleven of us girls are trying to study the Bible, but none of us are Christians. Do you know someone who could teach us the Bible?'"

From this contact, Sherri became involved in the lives of many college students in Bible study and witness, and a number became Christians and united with our church.

When God alerts you to where He is working, He intends for you to become involved with Him, so He can accomplish His will for others through your life.

But there is a further truth about applying, or living out, God's call in your life and responding to Him with sincere accountability! That is your INTERDEPENDENCE with other believers in the life of your church. Not only will they help you to know and clarify the will of God, or the call of God, in your life but they will also stand alongside of your life to assist you in fulfilling it. It is what I call divine interdependence. There are no loners in the living of the Christian life. We are mutually dependent upon each other. The New Testament describes this interdependence in the Christian life as life in the body of Christ. Three major Scripture passages help us to understand this clearly: Romans 12:3-8; 1 Corinthians 12:4-31; Ephesians 4:1-7,11-16. Paul strongly reminds the believers that they need each other, just as a body needs every part. He said, "You are the body of Christ, and each one of you is a part of it" (1 Cor. 12:27 NIV). And in Ephesians 4:13 (NIV) he reminds them that when each part in the body functions effectively where God has placed them, then the entire body grows up into the Head, which is Christ, until they "reach unity in the faith and in the knowledge of the Son of God and become mature, attaining to the whole measure of the fullness of Christ."

This will call for a joyful, willing ACCOUNTABILITY each to the other because we are all united to the Head, Jesus Christ. This was by divine plan. God would call us to Himself, but He would also with that call unite us with other believers in mutual love and accountability for the well-being of each other. It would be in the church that we encourage each believer to anticipate that God would work out their salvation call and take them on mission with Himself and others in their world. Expectation and anticipation become a way of life, and we are not disappointed.

In the church that I pastored we experienced together the excitement of being on mission. Ministry to the down-and-out people, to the school system, to the jails, to the mentally and physically handicapped, to the university, to the Indian reservations, to the surrounding towns and villages, and even to the ends of the earth was experienced by the members of our church. Everyone became involved, individually and together, with God in our world. Many felt called to be pastors or church staff people; other felt called to minister in other countries of the world; still others gained a clear sense of call to serve, witness, and minister in the marketplace and the homes where God had placed them. And together we helped each other to be ACCOUNTABLE—first to God Who had called us and to each other as we sought to be a body of Christ in our world through which the Father could carry out His purposes.

CONCLUSION

The call of God is a call to a total relationship with God for the purposes He had for us from before the foundation of the world. God calls us by causing us to want to do His will and then enabling us to do it. He first calls each of us to be a child of His by faith in Jesus, His Son. In that relationship God has provided all we need to live fully with Him. That relationship will always involve us in His redemptive activity in our world. In that relationship God Himself will work through us in our world. As God works through us in our world, we will come to know Him and grow toward Christlikeness. A Christlike character is God's preparation for eternity with Him. What a plan and what a purpose God has for each of us! May we respond to Him as He works in us and through us mightily in our world.

CALLED AND ACCOUNTABLE—God's greatest of privileges given freely to every believer!

Part 2

Called and Accountable
Journal

1: Daily we intentionally make calls to various persons in our lives. We have requests to make, news to share, or we want to catch up on how that person is doing. This accountability journal is designed to capture your dialogue with yourself about God's call in your life. Either the blank spaces in this book or your own journal will enable you to record your interaction with God's call in your life. You may have never spent much time thinking about His call, or your initial response. *Called and Accountable* is an invitation to explore and establish anew God's call and your maturing response to it. How do you express gratitude for being on the receiving end of God's call? Do you express gratitude?

2: At some time in each believer's life a light dawns that God is calling. Your call may lack the drama of Paul's Damascus Road experience. You may identify with young Samuel's call: He had to seek help from Eli in understanding what he was hearing and even Who was calling. Identify one early, specific time in your journey in which you sensed God's call. What do you recall? Where were you? Were you alone or with others? Describe yourself during this period of your life. Was there anything unique about you that the Almighty Creator God would call you?

3: A call involves a message and a response. God's earliest call to you was a declaration of His love through His Son, Jesus Christ. Your response to that call was a willingness to enter into a relationship with God. Reflect on your current relationship with Him. What do you know about God's call today that was unknown to you when you first responded? How would your life be different if you had ignored God's call? How has God's call caused you to stretch as a believer?

4: Your call is based on a relationship with Jesus Christ. Often relationships which are untended, like vegetable gardens, produce weeds, look unkempt, and cease yielding vegetables. Growth signs in a believer's life are straightforward and predictable: reading God's Word, praying, taking part in the church, and faith sharing. What are signs in your life which confirm to you that growth is occurring? Are you consciously aware of stages of growth that have occurred since your initial call to salvation? List them.

5: Since your initial call to salvation, ideally you have continued an ongoing dialogue with God. You are more sensitive to God's calls. Prayer and Bible study allow you to receive God's messages even in the midst of life in the fast lane. Whether you choose to record the interactions you have with God through keeping a journal, reflecting on them thoughtfully, or selecting an accountability prayer partner, how will you be able to assess next year the growth in your call from God?

6: Just as God initiated His call to you, you now have the opportunity to be a colaborer with God as He works in the world. How might the world be different if you were utterly serious about being God's instrument in the world today? Can you recall times when you have shrugged off or ignored God's call to you? When?

7: A response to God's call places some demands upon your life. *Obedience* is the operative word as a believer develops in knowledge of God and His ways. If words were categorized as hard and soft, *obedience* would be in the first category. Self-interest and personal comfort may obstruct our obedience to God. God's expectations are often startlingly clear and non-negotiable. What kind of personal adjustments have you made in order to be growing in your obedience to God? Why do some people describe the call of God as costly to the believer? Is it costly to you?

8: Someone has described character as the composite of our habits. One of the calls which God issues is that a believer develop the character of Christlikeness. If that particular call has been one which you have recognized, what are you doing about it? Identify some aspects of your character which are least Christlike. Can you imagine how God might direct you to change those habits? Name one specific change that you could initiate.

9: Many persons are uneasy when they are not in control. Relinquishing control does not necessarily mean that God will call you into the most uncomfortable or dangerous place of service. If control is important to you, imagine the most risk-filled call from God. What would it be in your life? Often you may be the only one who is aware that God is making a particular call. God is trusting you to respond. Can you refuse to be obedient and still face God? How?

10: God's call to salvation brought with it the gift of redemption. Subsequent calls which God makes to you involve the redemption of persons who do not know Him. Describe the life of a person who lives an authentically redemptive life. How is your life different from the one you have described? You may sense that God is calling for changes in your life that you are unwilling to consider. What are they? When will the time ever be right for you to consider those changes?

11: God does not call everyone to the vocation of formally appointed missionary. Is that a relief? That does not mean that the other calls He issues are of a lesser nature. God's plan from the beginning has been the redemption of the world. Even if you are not a vocational missionary, you have a role to fill in God's redemptive plan for the world. What is your initiative as an *influencer*, an *ambassador*, a *messenger*? You've heard those terms before. What do they mean to you in your sphere of influence?

12: God is the Great Initiator of all the significant calls in our lives. He provides through His Son a means by which all who will listen might hear and enter into a life-changing relationship. God's plan for the world involves the choice of human beings as His instruments. God chooses. God calls. God commissions. God's call is inclusive. As a believer, how do you model to others that openness which God extended to you? Do you assume any conscious responsibility for whether others hear God's call?

13: Human beings, created in God's image, have the opportunity to respond to God's call. There are some strings
attached to God's call. He expects believers to take off their
old selves and be willing to put on a new self (Col. 3:9). What
has this identity change meant in your pilgrimage? Identify
the vestiges of the you-before-you-heard-God calling that
remain the most troublesome for you. Is accepting God's call
worth this change?

14: The parable of the talents (Matt. 25:14-30) is one of
numerous scriptural reminders to the believer of the accountability which accompanies the acceptance of God's call. God
is willing to be an active participant in the living out of your
daily life. He created the life which you enjoy. You receive the
blessings of God. What is your strategy for allowing God to
be a full copartner in your daily decision making? When is it
easiest for you to acknowledge God's role in your life?

15: As a believer you are being led by God into deeper and deeper understandings about what His call means in your life. One aspect of His call is reflected in Romans 6:13. For much of society today, the concept of sin is ridiculed as old-fashioned. If your response to God is to offer yourself to Him as an imperfect but willing vessel for His righteousness' sake, what will others think? How important to you is the opinion of others about how you live your life? Does this affect your call or your accountability?

16: Every individual who hears a call has growth potential. That potential is God's gift to us. Someone has noted that what we choose to do with the potential is our gift to God. Undeveloped potential is wasting God's resources. Reflect on the diverse strengths and weaknesses which you have. Are you in the habit of rethinking your values and ambitions in God's presence? One of the merits of this accountability journal is that you maintain contact with your growth journey over a period of time. God encourages growth through all of our life circumstances. What are some ways you could fulfill your potential?

17: God is aware of the most minute part of His creation. The fall of one sparrow does not escape His attention. God's awareness of and purpose for your life has been in place long before you heard His call, long before you decided to cooperate with His call. When you consider your Creator's scrutiny of who you are, how you spend your time, the depth of your conversation with Him, how do you feel? Are there some resolutions which you would be willing to make that would strengthen your relationship with God?

18: A contemporary Christian song reminds us that God calls and uses "Ordinary People." The only catch is that the ordinary person must make herself or himself available to God. Do you ever think about what God could do with a person of abundant natural abilities, if that person was committed to God? If you are one of the many who categorizes themselves as middle-of-the-road and unexceptional beings, what might God want from you? Is your very ordinariness something you are willing to give to God?

19: Believers never outgrow God's calls. He may issue a new call or lead in a different direction. It is impossible to be selective in hearing the calls of God. The foundation of any call which is issued is *obedience*. God requires the lifelong obedience of his children. Sensitivity to God's calls and growth in obedience is expressed in your life as discipleship. What are you doing about your call to discipleship? If the test was today, how would you grade yourself on your discipleship?

20: God not only issues calls to believers but He expects that the individual will do a share of calling too. Isaiah 65:24 describes God's anticipation of your calls to Him. You may call on God in prayer as often as you choose. The Bible gives ample assurance that our calls to God not only please Him but bring answers. What "great and unsearchable things" has God revealed to you because you dared to call to Him? How up-to-date are your calls to God?

21: The Holy Spirit creates in each believer an inner awareness that facilitates a response to God's call. Often God's Spirit's role is one of nudging and encouraging you toward God's objective. The names of persons and ministry needs that seem to merely pop into your mind and toward which you feel called to respond are results of the work of the Spirit of God. How do you keep track of those needs to which you will respond? Making an intentional response is part of your accountability to God's call.

22: Perhaps the very basic tenet of Christianity is the doctrine of salvation. It is likely that several years have passed since you heard and responded to God's call to salvation. One of the challenges of Christian discipleship is to maintain a freshness regarding that life-changing call, not allowing the fervency and intentionality and gratitude for God's grace to become dim. The psalmist jubilantly declares in Psalm 27:1 that the Lord "is my light and my salvation." How does your call to salvation continue to bring light to your life today?

23: Children of God are on a continual growth journey from the moment in which they receive and respond to the call to salvation. God constantly places new calls in the lives of believers. These calls are unheard, unseen, and unfelt by all except those who are spiritually sensitive. Spiritual sensitivity enhances your ability to hear God. On a scale of one to ten, how would you rate your ability to hear God? Reflect on a recent situation in which you are reasonably certain that God was speaking. Do you need to improve your hearing?

24: Oftentimes God's calls are evident as we see God at work in the world around us. The frantic pace of life can block our awareness of God at work. Just as groups of persons go on retreat for spiritual purposes, perhaps you need a personal retreat to focus on how God is at work in your life, in your family's life, where you work, in your church, etc. A retreat does not have to last more than a few hours, but you need to find a distraction-free setting. You may not be ready to retreat. If you could, where would this place be? What would you hope might come from such a time with God?

25: A three-week-old baby would find little nourishment in the choicest cut of prime beef. Yet many adults would equate fine dining with that same entree selection. The difference? The maturity of the diner. How have you progressed since the stage in your life where spiritual milk was a necessity? Starting from the time you received Christ and considering your life in five-year increments, list some of the maturity milestones which you can identify (such as teaching a Sunday School class, sharing your faith, etc.).

26: Your sensitivity to God's calling you is increased as you continue to grow in your walk of faith. As a novice bicyclist learns to trust her sense of balance and sheds the training wheels, you are on a journey of learning to trust God. He never calls you by mistake or prematurely or casually. How are you trusting in the Lord with your whole heart as Proverbs 3:5 advises? Or, if your trust is only halfhearted, what will it take to make it unquestioning trust? Have you lived out your trust in God lately?

27: The stop sign on the corner is a simple, straightforward command. Most drivers comply with the sign, particularly when a policeman is in sight. Obedience to the call of God is trickier. Who is to know if you are compliant with what God is urging or encouraging you to do? There is little reward in boasting about your resistance to following God's direction. How effective or comfortable or frequent is your communication with God when you are being disobedient? Are there some descriptive terms you would choose other than *disobedience* when you are dragging your feet with God?

28: Thomas Merton has written, "The activity of the Spirit within us becomes more and more important as we progress in the life of interior prayer. . . . Our efforts [require] an increasingly attentive and receptive attitude toward the hidden action of the Holy Spirit." Your awareness of God's presence is heightened by a gift God provides for believers: His Holy Spirit. God's Spirit enables you to hear and know the call of God. Through gentle nudgings and occasional shoves the Spirit reminds us of God's plan for us. What has God been saying to you recently?

29: If your life leaves you gasping for breath as if you were competing in a marathon race, you may legitimately ask, How do you soar on wings like eagles, run and not grow weary, or walk and not faint? The answer may not be such a secret, but rather the act of appropriating the power of God's Spirit. This is simply God's plan. This is why you received the gift of the Spirit at the time of your salvation. List the major areas in your life in which you need to experience God's empowering Spirit.

30: A brief verse in Galatians (5:25) admonishes believers to keep in step with the Spirit. In a marching band every section of instruments needs to heed the direction of the same director. Likewise, believers are able to cooperate with God's plan by close attention to His Spirit. Consider the ups and downs of your spiritual life. What advice would you give to a new believer for keeping in step with the Spirit? Do you feel in or out of step with God's Spirit today?

31: God's Word is itself a call to missions, and through the guidance of His Spirit you can express your energy in implementing God's plan. Peter's bold declarations in the book of Acts occurred because he was filled with God's Spirit. Do you have a need or expectation for a similar boldness in your life? What differences would people who know you observe if suddenly you were more intensely in touch with God's empowering Spirit? Do you know how to tap into that power source?

32: God can use any circumstance or setting to engage your attention and issue a call. A believer who is intent upon seeking God's direction often tries out a variety of ministry activities. In the midst of leading a particular age group, or preparing or performing, God's call becomes more discernable. God seldom allows the luxury of complete isolation from activity as the primary setting for His call. What calls have you experienced in the midst of service? Do you need to intentionally place yourself in a new ministry setting?

33: Child development experts describe specific skills which children are able to perform at certain ages. There's a predictability about when children can stack blocks or identify colors or balance on a jungle gym. God is Himself your development expert. He assesses your growth and spiritual development. He does not call you to do a task for which you are unprepared. What characteristics of God enable you to trust His judgment in calling you? Has He ever led you into water over your head?

34: Have you ever forgotten a person's name? Or momentarily lost your sense of direction? The human memory has occasional lapses. Because God wants to ensure your success in obeying His calls, He has provided His Spirit to jog your memory. John 14:26 is one reminder about how you can depend on the Holy Spirit. How has the Spirit clarified or intensified God's calls to you? How could you practice relying on God's Spirit?

35: Logging in hours at an exercise club is likely to help you find a workout routine which stretches and tones your physique and builds your stamina. You are in an exercise-conducive setting. Your church has scheduled times of worship and teaching and ministry. Describe the relationships between your participation or involvement in your church and God's calls. How have you experienced God calling you through your church?

36: There may be many opportunities for you to lead through your church. It seems the busiest leaders are often the ones chosen for additional responsibilities. How does God enable you to discern which opportunity to serve is the best use of your gifts and skills? Someone has said, "Sometimes you have to say no in order to be free to say yes." Is every request for your leadership involvement a call from God? How do you tell?

37: There is not a single best translation of the phrase *involvement in missions*. You may be a long-term leader of a missions education organization. You may focus your energy on in-depth missions praying. Your involvement may be service-oriented toward society's outcasts. Your energies may be spent in energizing and equipping others through teaching. You may be able to give substantially to missions or feel led to volunteer your vacation time. You may be a dazzling study leader, or a faithful mentor to missionaries' kids (MKs). The translations are endless. There is a call involved in each one. Where do you fit today? Where would you like to fit?

38: God's Word is a rich resource for any believer who seeks God's ongoing call. Do you identify with Moses, who hearing God's call, countered with some earnest questions? Moses' question of "Who am I, that I should go?" may be yours. God is able to hear and respond to your deepest reservations or hesitancy about your call. What fears or concerns limit your willingness to be available to God? Voice those to Him in this journal.

39: Henry Blackaby has described prayer as the invitation of God to His people to keep oriented to His agenda. Your memory may be quite remarkable. For others writing in a daily prayer journal can remind you of the mile markers in your spiritual journey. God's calls to you begin to take shape as you reread the words you wrote two years ago or even last week. Today's prayer life is enriched as you consider God's faithfulness through your life circumstances. How has God affirmed His call to you through prayer in recent days?

40: Some family members bear a striking physical resemblance to each other. The family nose or eyes or chin is a resemblance link. As you become intent on being sensitive to God's call, you will find members of your church family who affirm that call. God uses other believers to nurture and call out those to whom He is calling. These persons confirm for you the authentic nature of your call. Reflect on a call which you have received. Who helped affirm that call and encouraged you? You have the opportunity to take on the role of encourager to others if your spiritual sensitivity is keen.

41: Consumers traditionally place a high value on satisfaction in the goods and services they purchase. An equivalent of consumer satisfaction is the personal peace and fulfillment guaranteed to the believer who is willing to follow God's call. Is your conversation time with God filled with excuses, rationalizations, and energy spent trying to modify what you sense God is calling you to do? How accurately does faithful obedience describe your spiritual walk? You alone are responsible for the unique calls He makes known to you.

42: The familiar exchange of "Let's keep in touch" between friends might mean a lengthy visit the next day or merely an annual Christmas card. Your regular times of conversation with God allow the relationship between you to develop. The habit of keeping in touch with God is an intentional act on the believer's part. Convenience or whether you feel like it ought not be primary considerations. Do you keep in touch with God as often as you read the daily newspaper or watch television? Talk to God about the hindrances to your daily relationship with Him.

43: Too often a middle-of-the night telephone call is news of an illness, death, or other emergency circumstance. You are immediately awake and anxious to respond. While God's calls may arrive at any hour that you are in tune with Him, the necessary response is similar—immediate awareness and willingness to obey. Have you ever adjusted your life in a radical way in order to respond to God? What new radical adjustment do you sense that God is calling for?

44: Some people are in the habit of making decisions by listing the pros and cons of an action. If the positives outnumber the negatives, then the action is taken. God's calls are not negotiable. He seldom, if ever, issues a call with a multiple-choice response. How can you know? God's Word provides deep and eternal truths about Him. How is the amount of time spent in studying and meditating on God's Word related to your decision making? List Scripture verse(s) which have served as guiding verses for you in responding to God's call.

45: In baseball several coaches are accessible to the players. The baseline coach provides instructions and signals for the player who may be too caught up in the immediate task of reaching home plate to make accurate on-the-spot judgments. God's coach for believers is His Spirit. One of the ways you hear and know God's will and calls is through God's Spirit. How do you plan to grow in sensitivity to the nudging of the Spirit? What role does the Spirit have in your life's game plan?

46: Birthdays, Thanksgiving, and Christmas celebrations are often times of high expectations. The sheer anticipation heightens the joy. God's Word provides ample assurance that He has a long-range plan for His creation. What's your level of excitement about what God has in store for you? God's plan is based on His sovereignty and power. His plan makes provision for each and every one who is willing to respond to His call. How does the assurance that the Almighty God has a plan especially for your life make you feel? Does your expectation of God's ability to carry out His plan waver at times? How do you counter your doubts?

47: Have you ever considered intentionally looking for where God is working and joining Him in His work? As you grow in sensitivity to the signs that God is leading in your life, it makes sense to live out the spirit of 1 Corinthians 3:9 and become an authentic colaborer with God. God's divine direction is surely preferable to any other plan, no matter how appealing. List several areas in your life in which God is at work. How could you be more cooperative with God's plan? Will you?

48: Believers who are by nature activists may struggle with remaining still, even though they are unsure about which direction God would have them go. Movement in any direction seems preferable to waiting. At times, though, God's call is to linger or pause where you are. In His timing the next appropriate move will be revealed. How do you evaluate your willingness to await God's direction? Can you recall a truth that God has taught you through waiting? Reflect on Psalm 130:5.

49: Just as wise parents teach their children the meaning of responsible behavior, God teaches His children about the stewardship of life which He expects. The variety of calls which God issues to you are your invitation to respond. God is the only One Who keeps track of your responses. Hebrews 4:13 relates to God's omniscience. Describe your willingness to have God scrutinize your accountability to His calls. How is your attitude? Joyful? Willing? Could it be improved?

50: One of the great benefits of keeping a spiritual journal is looking back at where you were a month ago or five years ago. As your self-awareness grows, talents that God has given to you emerge. More importantly, your use of those talents is readily accessible through scanning the written pages of your personal journal, your written interaction with God about your willingness to obey Him. How does your life exhibit your growing sensitivity to God? Do you have some desire or plans for growth in the future?

51: Have you ever uttered a sincere "Let me know if there's anything I can do" to another person? You were making your time and energy available to be responsive to the needs of that individual. Availability has its price tag. You may be called upon at a highly inconvenient time, or asked to render a service which is not one with which you are comfortable. Availability is God's call to the mature believer. If one end of a believer's spiritual spectrum is availability to God, the other end would necessarily be personal control. How close to being totally available to God are you? Do you want to be?

52: Once you are aware that God's calls are ongoing and continual, you begin to look for God's presence in every aspect of your life. If you have been one to relegate your spiritual dialogue to a prescribed time in the morning or evening, are you excited about the possibility of discovering Him in even the mundane aspects of your life? In a spiritual classic, *Practice of the Presence of God*, Brother Lawrence discovered a keen sense of God's nearness as he peeled potatoes in the monastery kitchen. Does your agenda include some potato peeling today? Your accountability to respond includes calls God will issue according to His schedule. Look for Him in even the predictable and repetitious moments of your schedule. He's there. Calling. And you are accountable.

TEACHING PLAN

Preparation
1. Read the entire teaching plan and note all of the items to be prepared before the study.
2. Enlist any workers you will need to assist with the study.
3. Purchase copies of the book *Called and Accountable* for each participant or arrange for participants to purchase the books prior to or at the study (books available through Baptist Book Stores). Remember, to obtain Church Study Course credit, participants must read the book and complete the 2 1/2 hours of class study. To fulfill individual option, individuals must complete the accountability journal.

Introductory Activities (10 minutes)
Choose one of the following activities.

*Copy the title page of *Called and Accountable* for every two participants you expect to attend the study. Cut the copies in half using a distinct zigzag pattern for each sheet.

When participants enter the room for the study, give each one half of a title page. Instruct them to mingle with other study participants to locate the matches for their sheets. After matches are located, ask partners to tell *(a)* one thing they feel called to do and *(b)* at least three people to whom they are accountable.

*Post a sign on one side of the room which reads *I Am Called to* _____. Post a second sign on the other side of the room which reads *I Am Accountable to* _____. As participants enter, ask them to stand beneath one of the two signs and discuss how they would finish the statement.

Study Activities
The study can be presented using a flip chart or an overhead projector. The statements in boldface should be copied on the flip chart or on overhead cells in the order in which they are presented here. To complete the activities using the numbered journal entries, you may refer participants to the

book or copy the referenced entries and distribute as hand-outs.

1. **What It Means to Be Called and Accountable.** Introduce the study and the book. Assign participants to read Romans 1:6; 1 Corinthians 1:1-2; Ephesians 1:1-6,18; 4:1; 1 Thessalonians 1:4; 2 Thessalonians 1:11. Ask participants to list the terms used to denote "called."

2. **Why does God call us?** Review the introduction. Reveal each of the responses to the question as each point is discussed: **(1) To accomplish His purposes in the world; (2) to prepare us for eternity; (3) to develop character.**

3. **Chapter 1: "What Is a Call?"** Refer participants to journal entry 2. Ask participants to select partners and answer the questions raised in this entry.

4. **Relationship.** Review the section on relationship on page 5. Ask participants to recall biblical examples of God pursuing the relationship of love. Record responses on flip chart or overhead. Refer participants to journal entry 4. Ask them to reflect and respond silently to this entry.

5. **Redemptive.** Review section. Tell stories of individuals who identified and followed God's call to be on mission.

6. **"Every Christian is called of God to salvation, and in that same call is the call to be on mission with God in our world. This is what it means to be called."** Ask participants if they agree or disagree with this statement. Discuss responses.

7. **"In every generation, in every place He saves some, develops them as His children, and takes them on mission with Him in their world. This is what it means to be called."** Ask participants if they agree or disagree with this statement. Review material on pages 7 and 8.

8. **Assignment/Invitation/Appointment.** Review the points regarding God's assignment to Noah, his invitation to Moses, and his appointment of the disciples.

9. **Missions volunteers.** Write to Volunteers in Missions (Foreign Mission Board, P. O. Box 6767, Richmond, VA 23230; or Home Mission Board, 1350 Spring Street, NW, Atlanta, GA 30367) for a list of the current needs. Review the needs. Read the names on the prayer calendar for the day of the study. Ask participants to list items that career missionaries may

have to forfeit in order to serve God on their missions field. Option: Ask an individual in your church who has served as a missions volunteer to share his or her testimony.

10. **Obedience always accompanies God's call.** Refer participants to journal entry 7. Ask individuals to respond silently.

11. **"A call always involves the person in the corporate life of the people of God."** Review how your church supports missionaries. Read journal entry 11 aloud. Ask participants to respond to the questions.

12. **Chapter 2: "Who Are the Called?"** Lead a group discussion of journal entry 12. Provide an overview of chapter 2.

13. **Ordinary People.** Obtain a list of service opportunities in your community and/or through your church. Post or distribute this list as the stories of Arthur and Marion and Melvin are told. Allow time for private reflection of journal entry 18.

14. **Taught/Trained/Guided/Encouraged/Empowered/Equipped.** List the words, so that they can be revealed one at a time. Refer to page 14 and John 17 as you discuss how Jesus worked with His disciples then and how He accomplishes these tasks today.

15. **Responding to God's call.** Ask each participant to complete a list of needs and responses using journal entry 21 as a guide.

16. **Chapter 3: "How Am I Called?"** Tell how you have felt God's call in your life. Or enlist others to tell of their experiences.

17. **"Yes, Lord!"** Discuss the impact of saying yes to the lordship of Christ. Instruct participants to find a partner and work through journal entry 23 together.

18. **Hear and Follow/See and Join/Understand and Obey.** As each point is revealed to the group, read the related Scripture verses (see p. 17).

19. **Preparing for God's call.** Discuss the points made on page 17 related to experiencing the fullness of God's call. Prepare strip posters using the first sentence of the enumerated points and reveal each statement as you discuss it. Lead participants to complete journal entry 25 silently.

20. **Creating the atmosphere.** Pages 17 and 18 speak of cre-

ating a spiritual atmosphere at church and at home. Brainstorm ideas on how this can be done.

21. **Chapter 4: "When Am I Called?"** Ask participants to share their responses to journal entry 32 with partners.

22. **At the time of the call/As a result of the call.** Divide your flip chart or overhead into two columns with these headings. Using the Scripture references on page 21, ask participants to determine what each of the examples (Moses and elders, Judges, David, etc.) were doing at the time of the call and the results. Complete the chart.

23. **"The Spirit-filled life was to be God's normal life for the Christian."** Review the Scripture verses on page 21 related to the Holy Spirit's role in the life of one who is called.

24. **"The loving Christ is truly present in the church body, and each member really does assist the others to know and do the will of God."** As you discuss the role of the church in the life of the called (last paragraph on p. 21), ask participants to respond to journal entry 40 aloud.

25. **(List the four points provided in the last paragraph of chap. 4.)** Discuss journal entry 38 as you reveal point 1 and journal entry 39 as you reveal point 2. Ask for private reflection of journal entry 37 as you reveal point 3. Encourage partners to respond to journal entry 35 after revealing point 4.

26. **Chapter 5: "How Do I Live Out the Call?"** Discuss journal entry 44 and list the Scripture verses participants share as guiding verses.

27. **(List the three major points of the chapter.)** Using the three responses to the chapter's question as an outline, review the content.

28. **"God calls us by causing us to want to do His will and then enabling us to do it."** Lead participants to engage in a silent reflection and commitment time by referring them to journal entries 47 and 48.

29. As a conclusion, ask participants to share with someone close by how they plan to be more accountable to God's call. Close with a short prayer.